The creatur[illegible]ed with rage an[illegible] [illegible] hand clutched a jeweled knife. Each step he took toward Don brought him closer to revenge. Don stumbled backward, trying to escape his relentless advance.

You are the one who made me to look like a hideous monster. You shall pay! I shall have my revenge!

Don fell backward. The creature, his hateful, deformed face gloating in final triumph, lifted the knife. Don saw the yellow teeth and blackened lips twist into a dreadful smile.

The only sound Don heard in the silent tomb was his own scream.

RETURN TO THE TOMB OF DEATH

by Alida E. Young

To my husband Pete—
for all his help, encouragement, and support

Cover illustration by Richard Kriegler

Published by Worthington Press
7099 Huntley Road, Worthington, Ohio 43085

Printed in the United States of America
10 9 8 7 6 5 4 3 2 1

ISBN 0-87406-455-4

Contents

CHAPTER 1

The Cobra Medallion

DONOVAN Hunt lay on his bed, watching the storm clouds gather outside his window. He was just getting over the flu. The sky was getting darker by the minute, and the clouds were being whipped around by the wind. The trees looked like they were bent over as far as they could go without snapping. It looks like there's going to be a real storm, he thought.

He dropped the sports magazine he was reading and stared out the window. Something about the wild storm approaching made Don think about the locked wooden box on his dresser. He hadn't opened the box for several months—he had been afraid to. But he had thought about what was in there a hundred times a day since he got back from Egypt.

But now, something was drawing him to the

box, almost like a voice that he had to obey. Don's heart beat faster, and his breath caught in his throat as he reached toward the box. As his hand put the key in the lock, a jagged flash of lightning ripped across the sky, followed by a tremendous boom of thunder.

Don dropped the key. His hand was shaking.

"This is really stupid," he told himself with a nervous laugh. "What am I afraid of? I'm here in my room in New York. Nothing can happen to me here."

Don took a deep breath and unlocked the box. He reached in and pulled out a small stone medallion on a ribbon. He held it in his hand as the thunder and lightning crashed outside his window.

There was a cobra etched on one side of the medallion. On the other side of the medallion was the Eye of Horus, an ancient Egyptian god who looked like a hawk. When he was in the museum in Cairo, Egypt, Don had seen another medallion like this one. The only difference between the two medallions was that the one in the museum had a falcon on it instead of a cobra.

But both medallions had a strange power. Whenever Don stared into the Eye of Horus when he was in Egypt, he went into a kind of trance. He was able to see things that happened a long time ago—as if he was really there!

But now, as he held the medallion here in his room at home in New York, all that seemed a long way away. The medallion couldn't have the same power here, he thought. Like his grandfather said, strange things happen in the deserts of Egypt. But this was New York! Weird things like that just didn't happen here.

Don took the medallion back to his bed. He propped up his pillows so he could watch the storm. He held the medallion in his hand. As the storm grew wilder, Don fought the urge to stare into the Eye of Horus. But something was drawing him to it.

He held the medallion up and looked at it. He looked deep into the eye of the ancient god, across the ocean to the desert sands and back though the centuries to long ago.

Don saw a crowded marketplace, filled with people wearing long robes with hoods that covered their faces. There was a young boy hurrying through the crowd. He came to a stall of some kind, and an old man came out. The old man started to beat the boy with a stick, and the boy cried and whimpered like a hurt animal. The old man pulled off the boy's hood and started to hit him on the head.

Don saw with horror that the boy looked just like him!

Don woke from his trance and screamed.

"Don! What's wrong?"

He looked up and saw his grandfather in the doorway of his room. He looked like a big friendly bear with a bushy white beard. Don always felt safe with him, and his panic slowly disappeared.

"I—I guess I was just having a bad dream," Don said. "Maybe I still have a little fever."

"Were you thinking about the mummy your folks discovered in Egypt?"

Don nodded and looked over at the picture of the mummy on his wall. "Yeah, Grandpa Pete," he answered, "I guess I was. That and other stuff."

Don's friends all envied him because his mom and dad were archaeologists. But sometimes it wasn't so great. Ever since they were kidnapped and almost killed in Egypt, Don worried about his mom and dad all the time when they were away. Now his parents were in Thailand looking for a giant gold statue. Don's grandmother was with his parents, too, and Grandpa Pete was staying with him in New York to write a book about his discoveries.

"I think about the mummy a lot," Don continued in a quiet voice. "I have nightmares about him. I can still see his horrible eyes. And when he touched me..." Don shuddered.

"Look, Don," said Grandpa, sitting down on the edge of Don's bed. "Try not to think too much about it. That mummy was just one of those terrorists dressed in a costume."

"I know there was a man dressed like a mummy. But the mummy that came up the elevator in the Red Tulip Hotel wasn't like any person dressed up in a costume. He seemed so real." Don sighed. "Oh, what's the use? Nobody believes me."

"There are plenty of things in this world that we don't understand," said Grandpa. "Nobody believed your grandmother and me when we were studying zombies in Haiti and we found that rare plant that could make a person appear to be dead."

"Yeah, but that doesn't sound as crazy as a mummy coming to life and chasing me around Cairo."

"Well, you're safe here, son." Grandpa Pete patted Don's shoulder and noticed the medallion. "Did you bring back any other souvenirs from Egypt?"

"Just my green scarab beetle with the Gemini horoscope on it. An old man shoved it into my hand in the marketplace."

His grandfather laughed. "I'll bet he said it was guaranteed to be from King Tut's tomb."

"No. He was a weird, creepy old guy, and he said it came from the tomb that Mom and Dad discovered. I know it sounds crazy, but he seemed to know who I was. Then he told me to leave Egypt. He said I was in danger from the past."

"The only danger you're in is from me if you don't stop thinking about Egypt and mummies." His grandfather pretended to sound gruff. "So just knock it off, and stay in bed. Your flu is almost gone. If you take it easy for one more day, you will be fine."

Don sighed again. "Okay, Grandpa. I'll try." His grandfather went out and shut the door.

Don hated being sick in the summer. It was such a drag not being able to go out and mess around with his friends. He tried to forget about his horrible vision of the beaten boy who looked like him. He tried to read about his favorite baseball team, the New York Mets. But he couldn't concentrate on the story. His mind kept wandering back to Egypt and everything that had happened to him there at the beginning of the summer.

He saw the medallion on his bed where he

had dropped it when he screamed. Without looking at the Eye of Horus, he walked over and put the medallion back in the box.

He felt a little weak and tired, so he crawled back into bed and pulled the covers over his face to keep out the flashes of lightning. Soon, he drifted off to sleep.

He took a step into the tomb. Thick black silence was all around. He swallowed nervously. He was soaked in icy sweat. He played his flashlight over the stone floor...and shrieked.

Mummies, skeletons, bones, and skulls lay in scattered piles! The flashlight dropped from his sweaty fingers. The light went out. There was total darkness. He started to back out but he heard a loud thud. The heavy door to the tomb had closed.

He was sealed in the chamber of death!

Don awoke, gasping for breath. He struggled to get free of the covers wrapped around his face. Although the room was hot and humid, he shivered. He could still remember how it had felt to be locked in that awful tomb.

Don was still trying to get his horrible dream out of his mind when his grandfather opened the door quietly.

"It's okay," Don said. "Come on in. I'm awake."

"The mail just came. I thought you'd want to read this."

"Is it a letter from Mom and Dad?" Don asked excitedly.

"No." His grandfather held out a long envelope. "It's from your friend Ali in Cairo."

"All right!" shouted Don. "It's about time. I've written him four letters since I got home."

Don glanced at the Red Tulip Hotel stationery, and then tore open the envelope. Even though they'd only seen each other during two summer vacations, Ali was one of his best friends. Don began to read the letter.

Dear Dono:

Sorry I haven't written sooner, but I've been really busy. Grandfather has been sick, so I've been doing my job as bellboy and also running the elevator for him.

But here's the big news! I have to tell you this. It's too important to wait. Dono, I think I've seen your twin!

"Grandpa Pete, don't leave!" Don said as his grandfather was headed out the door. "Listen to this. It's about my twin. Ali's seen him!"

Don's grandfather plopped down on the bed. He looked a little dazed. "I can't believe it! For 15 years, your mom and dad have searched for him. Ali must be mistaken."

Don had known he was adopted since he was five. But it was only a few months ago that he had learned that his parents had found him abandoned in a cave in the Valley of the Kings in Egypt. Villagers had mentioned another baby boy, but no record of him was ever found.

Don went on to read the letter out loud.

I passed a boy dressed in rags. He looked up, and I nearly fell over. I thought it was you—the same green eyes, hawklike nose, and high cheekbones. You know, just like pictures of the Pharaohs. I mean, Dono, this guy was you—no doubt about it! For a second I was really mad to think you had come back to Egypt without telling me. But then I realized that it couldn't be you.

I started to say something to him, but an old man grabbed him and started beating him with a stick. I think your mom and dad should get over here right away.

Grandpa Pete didn't say anything for a minute. Then he said in a low, serious voice, "I think we'd better check this out. I'll try to call your parents right now." He walked out of Don's room.

Still holding the letter, Don stared at the rain beating against the window. His mind was going around and around. All he could think was, My twin, my brother is alive!

Then an incredible thought struck him.

The medallion! He had seen his twin in the medallion! He didn't know how or why, but the ancient medallion had shown him his twin brother being beaten in the marketplace, just like Ali's letter said. The hair on the back of his neck stood up, and Don felt a cold shiver all over his body.

He decided not to tell his grandfather about what he had seen in the medallion. Grandpa might think he was still sick and not let him go to Egypt. Don reread the letter several times, just to make sure of what it said. Then he went to the study to see if his grandfather had gotten through to Thailand.

Grandpa Pete was still on the phone. "Yes...yes, I understand," he was saying. "But as soon as they return to Bangkok, please give them a message to call the Red Tulip Hotel in Cairo, Egypt. It's extremely important!"

His grandfather slammed down the phone. "They've gone to the jungles in northern Thailand and can't be reached. Pack your bags, Don. We're going to Egypt to find your twin!"

CHAPTER 2

A Living Mirror

AFTER a very hectic 48 hours of packing, shopping, and traveling, Don and his grandfather landed in the ancient city of Cairo. On the ride from the airport to the hotel, Don stared out the window of the taxi. Now that he knew he was Egyptian by birth, he found himself looking at the city with new eyes.

The taxi inched its way through narrow streets teeming with men in *galabias,* long striped robes, and women in long black veils. Honking trucks belched black smoke. The taxi passed noisy buses jammed with passengers hanging onto the sides. The taxi almost ran over sheep and donkeys and camels.

Grandpa Pete fanned himself with a newspaper. "Whew! I always forget how hot Cairo is in the summer."

The taxi pulled up in front of the Red Tulip

Hotel, and Don and his grandfather got out. His parents had been coming to the old hotel for years. Here, everybody made them feel like members of the family.

Ali came running forward to take their bags. He was wearing the traditional turban and a galabia. But instead of the usual sandals, Ali was wearing the high-top athletic shoes that Don had given him on the last trip.

"Dono! It's great to see you again." Ali gave him a bear hug, and then kissed him on both cheeks, in the Egyptian manner. Then he added, "These shoes you gave me look totally rad, don't they, my man!"

Don laughed. Ali knew as much American slang as any kid Don knew in New York. He learned it from TV and tourists. "I never thought I'd be coming back to Egypt so soon," Don said, giving Ali a friendly punch on the shoulder.

As Ali took them to their rooms on the fifth floor, he told them again about seeing the boy who looked exactly like Don.

"I don't even want to unpack before we go look for him," Don said, waiting for Ali to open the doors to the rooms where they always stayed.

"I think I'll lie down for a while before dinner," Grandpa Pete said. "My sore knee is acting up again. It's hard to sit still for so long on the plane."

Don frowned in disappointment. "But by then it'll be too late to go to the bazaar."

"We'll go first thing in the morning when it's cooler," his grandfather said. "I promise."

"May I bring you some tea, Grandpa Hunt, sir?" Ali asked him.

Grandpa Pete shook his head. "No thanks, Ali. Just be sure to wake me up for dinner, please." Ali opened the door to Grandpa Pete's room and set his bag inside. "See you later, boys," Grandpa said. "Don't get into any trouble."

Ali opened the door to Don's room down the hall and set the bag inside. "Come on in, if you have time," Don said. "I have something for you."

Don opened his suitcase and handed a small instant flash camera to Ali.

"Oh, Dono, it's great. This is the kind where you can see the photo right after you take it, isn't it?"

Don grinned. "That's right. We'll have fun with that."

"But it's too much," Ali said. "You gave me presents last time."

"This is from Mom and Dad—a thank you for all you did for me."

"I never in a million years thought I'd own a camera," Ali said.

Don knew that Ali only made about 25 cents per day on tips. He'd have to work for years and years to afford a camera.

"How come your parents aren't here?" asked Ali after he had looked at the camera for a while.

"They're in Thailand, looking for a giant gold Buddha. We couldn't get in touch with them. But, hey, what about my twin? Have you seen him a second time? Did he really look like me?"

"Hey, one question at a time. No, I didn't go back to the bazaar because your twin and the old guy would have recognized me. Remember, our pictures were in the paper. I was afraid I might scare them away before you got here. And, yeah, he sure does look like you, except he's a lot thinner."

Don jumped up. "I can't wait until tomorrow. I want to try to find him now. Can you get off work?"

"Sure thing. I'm not going to let you go alone. Your twin probably doesn't speak English."

"Thanks, Ali. Let's go!"

"You'd better wear one of my galabias. Then you won't stand out so much."

While Ali hurried off to get the galabia and turban, Don took the medallion from his pocket and put it around his neck. In a minute, Ali was back with the clothes. Don changed and they slipped down the dark stairwell.

Ali hailed a taxi to take them to the markets in the Old City. Don couldn't remember ever having been so excited or nervous. His hands were sweating so much that he almost dropped the money when he paid the driver.

They entered one of the narrow alleys lined with hundreds of little stalls.

"I saw him in a stall near the spice bazaar," Ali said. "He was selling glass trinkets."

As he followed Ali, Don walked slower and slower. The heat was even worse in the crowded, airless alleys. Sweat dripped from his forehead. "Maybe Grandpa Pete was right. Maybe we should come back tomorrow morning when it's cooler."

"Are you sure? We're almost there."

Don came to a full stop. "Ali?"

"What's wrong, Dono?"

"I don't know exactly. What if he isn't my brother, after all? Or what if it is him and he doesn't want anything to do with me? What if I don't like him? He might be weird or something. And if Mom and Dad adopt him, my whole life will be different. I guess I'm just kind of scared. I want to see him, but..."

Ali touched his arm. "Hey, Dono, we can go back to the hotel if you want to."

Don shook his head and took a deep breath. "I have to know if he's really my twin. Let's go."

As they neared the spice bazaar with its odors of ginger and cinnamon, Don saw a stall that sold trinkets and souvenirs. But it was all closed up, with a tarp pulled down over the front of the stall.

"Oh, no!" shouted Don. "They're gone!"

"Let me go up and take a look," said Ali. "You wait here."

Don watched as Ali walked over to the closed-up stall. What if he had come all this way only to miss seeing his brother?

But his heart leaped when he saw Ali break into a big grin. He was pointing to a piece of paper that had been pinned to the tarp. Ali motioned, and Don ran over to the stall.

"Great news, Dono," said Ali. "This says in Arabic that the stall is closed today. But they're going to be open tomorrow as usual."

"I wonder if I can wait!"

"Well, my man," answered Ali with a smile, "you don't have any choice. Let's go back to the Red Tulip."

When they got back to the hotel, Don realized how tired he was from the plane trip, the heat, and the tension about maybe seeing his brother. He fell asleep right away in his room and slept through dinner. When he woke up in the evening, he found that Ali had left him some food on a tray. Don ate the food and went back to sleep.

He awoke the next morning feeling refreshed and ready to go. The first thing he thought was, Today is the day I'm going to find out about my brother. He got up and went down to Grandpa Pete's room.

"Come on in," said Grandpa.

Don saw his grandfather sitting in a chair with his leg up on the bed. There was a towel wrapped around his knee. "I'm afraid I won't be going anywhere," he said. "I need to stay off my knee for a day. I think it will be fine tomorrow."

Grandpa Pete saw the disappointment on Don's face, and he said, "Don't worry. You can still go down to the bazaar to have a look around. But go with Ali, and be very careful."

"All right, Grandpa Pete! I'll be careful. I hope your knee feels better!" Don shouted as he ran out of the room to find Ali.

After breakfast, Don and Ali took a taxi to the market. Don had changed into his galabia. They found their way to the aisle where they had seen the closed stall. It was open this time, like the note had promised.

An old man was working at a table in the back. A sign in English said HOROSCOPES. THIS IS YOUR LUCKY DAY.

"That's the place," Ali said. "But I don't see the boy."

Don suddenly gripped Ali's arm and drew him back out of sight of the old man. "I was here two months ago," Don whispered. "That's the same stall where the old guy gave me the carved scarab beetle with my horoscope on it. He warned me to leave Egypt. I thought he was a mind reader or something when he knew my birth sign."

They watched the man helping customers for a while. Then a terrible thought struck Don. "What if that guy's my father, my *real* father?" he said to Ali.

"I don't think so," answered Ali. "He looks too old to be your father."

"He could be my grandfather."

The old man moved out of sight.

"What should we do?" asked Don.

"We could go back..."

Just then, a boy dressed in rags came from behind the stall. Don stared. It was him—his own twin! It was like looking into a living mirror.

"He's so thin," Don whispered to Ali. "And look at those awful bruises on his face!"

Don walked slowly toward the stall. "Don, wait," whispered Ali. But Don didn't hear him and kept on walking in a daze.

The other boy saw him and dropped a tray of scarab beetles. The two stared at each other for a moment. Don started forward to speak to his twin. But the boy shook his head, warning Don away. The old man was still behind the stall.

"Ali," Don said as he returned to where Ali was waiting. "Will you write a note to the boy for me in Arabic?"

Ali pulled out a scrap of paper and pencil. "What should I write?" he asked.

"Ask him to come to the Red Tulip Hotel," Don said. Ali scribbled a note and handed it to Don. Folding it until it was small, Don walked by and casually dropped it near the stall. Just as the other boy leaned down to pick it up, the old man came out from behind the stall. He said something in Arabic and began to strike the boy with a stick.

Horrified, Don watched the vision he had scene in his bedroom when he stared into his medallion in New York! He started to rush forward, but Ali grabbed his arm. "You can't interfere in a family argument, Dono."

"Family argument?" Don shouted. "I'm that kid's family! I'm his brother!"

"We'll come back with help. We shouldn't have come here without your grandfather."

It took all Don's control not to go help his brother, but Ali was right. Don wanted to shout to his twin, Don't worry. You'll soon be safe!

Don followed Ali as they left the bazaar. On the way out, neither one said much. They were looking for a taxi when they heard the sound of footsteps behind them. They turned to see Don's twin running toward them with a terrified look on his face.

CHAPTER 3

The Grave Robber Has Many Friends

"HELP me!" the twin cried in English. "Abdul is after me!"

"Follow me," Ali said. "I know the city." The three of them raced through alleys and small streets, trying to avoid bumping into camels and donkeys and carts filled with fruit.

After they had been running for about a half an hour, Don said, "Let's take a rest. I don't see how that old man could have followed us through this crowd."

Don's twin kept looking back. "Abdul has many friends. They will catch me." He shuddered and touched the bruises on his face.

Don hated to see the fear in his brother's eyes. "Don't worry," he whispered. "We won't let them get you."

Ali was looking at an old mud brick house. Some of the bricks had broken loose. "Come on," Ali said.

They climbed to the roof, using the broken bricks as toeholds. "The buildings are so close together we can jump from roof to roof," Ali explained.

Before Don jumped across to the next building, he pulled up his galabia. "This would be a lot easier if I wasn't wearing this darned nightgown," he said.

"At least we have the right shoes," said Ali pointing to his high tops that matched Don's. Don was about to laugh until he noticed that his twin was staring at Ali's shoes. Don felt ashamed and sad when he saw that his brother wore only a ragged pair of old leather sandals. Things will be different when we're back home together, Don told himself.

They raced across the roofs. Don felt like a huge cat leaping between buildings. Even his twin looked more excited than scared now. When they were in sight of the Red Tulip Hotel, they stopped to rest. Don stared at his twin. It was like looking in a mirror, except for the bruises and the thinness of the other's face.

Don said, "I'm Donovan Hunt. And this is my friend Ali."

His twin nodded. "I know. I saw your pictures in the paper. I am called Ben-Seyad." He looked nervously around. "I should not have followed you. Now, Abdul-Habib and his friends will hurt you, too."

"We'll hide you," Don said. "My grandfather will know what to do."

"But what if Abdul is already at the hotel?" Ben-Seyad asked. "He read your note."

"We'll watch the building to see who goes in," Ali said. "Then when it's dark, we'll jump across to the Tulip's roof. It's right across this alley. That's where I live—on the roof in that little house over there, next to my grandfather's chicken cages. I hope you're good jumpers, though. It'll be the longest jump yet."

The boys sat on the roof and rested after their long escape. Don saw that Ben-Seyad kept staring at him. He must know that we're twins, thought Don.

A line of washing flapped in the breeze above their heads. Don couldn't help noticing that Ben-Seyad squatted on the ground, like he was ready to run away.

"Is Abdul your father?" Don asked. He hated to think he might be related to that evil old man.

"I have no parents," Ben-Seyad answered. "When I was a baby, someone found me outside a cave and took me to a village. The woman who raised me is dead. Abdul bought me after she died. He treats me like his slave."

"Where do you live?" asked Ali.

"We live near the Valley of the Kings, close to the tomb your parents discovered," Ben-Seyad said. He turned to Don. "When Abdul saw your picture in the paper, he guessed you and I must be related. He decided to get a lot of money from your parents by selling me to them, because we are related. He hates your parents."

"Why?" Don wanted to know. "What did they do to him?"

"Abdul is a grave robber. He was robbing a tomb on the other side of the mountain from where your parents found the mummy of a prince. When your parents started working in the tomb, Abdul and the others had to stop their own digging."

"Who's buried there?" asked Don "My mom and dad will want to know about this."

"Some priest-vizier named Ahmeket," answered Ben-Seyad. "He was only the pharaoh for a short time."

Ali shook his head. "I've read a lot of history books, but I've never heard of him." When Ben-Seyad looked surprised, Ali said, "I want to be an archaeologist, so I study our ancient history whenever I can."

Don poked Ali's arm. "This is the smartest guy I know. He speaks a bunch of languages and is even learning to read hieroglyphics!"

"You speak English well," Ali said to Ben-Seyad.

"I learned English from talking to tourists when I sell them things."

Keeping watch on the hotel entrance, they talked for a while longer. "It's getting dark," Ali said. "I haven't seen any strangers go into the hotel. I think it's safe to jump across now."

The three stood looking at the distance between the buildings. To Don it looked at least six feet. Ali jumped first. His grandfather's chickens in their cages started squawking when Ali landed on the hotel roof.

Then Ben-Seyad leaped across. As he landed on the other side, he gave a muffled cry.

"What's wrong?" Don called.

"I cut my arm on a piece of metal," Ben-Seyad said. "It is nothing."

"Move to your left, Dono, so you'll miss the metal," Ali said.

Don looked down the six stories to the alley below. He got a good running start, and leaped. But his foot caught in his galabia, and his jump was too short. Wildly, frantically his fingers reached for the wall on other side. But he felt only air.

CHAPTER 4

The Magic of the Medallion

HIS heart beating wildly, Don reached for the edge of the roof. His hand grabbed the ledge. He tried to hold on, but his fingers started to slip.

Ali grabbed one arm, and Ben-Seyad grabbed the other. "We've got you," Ali said.

Then Ben-Seyad said in a whisper, "Shhh! Abdul is in the alley!"

Don tried to look down.

"Dono, don't move. Maybe he won't look up."

Silently, Don dangled in mid-air. His arms felt as if they were being pulled from the sockets. He wondered how long Ali and Ben-Seyad could hold onto him.

After what seemed to Don like hours, Ali said, "It's okay. He's gone."

Slowly, they pulled Don up until his shoulders were above the edge of the roof. He rested a moment, and then his twin and Ali brought him up the rest of the way. He fell in a heap, too scared and exhausted to move.

Ben-Seyad leaned over Don. "Are you all right?" he asked.

Don sat up. His insides still felt empty. "Yeah, but that was a close call." He noticed blood on his brother's arm. "But, hey, you're the one who's hurt."

"It is nothing," he answered.

Don tore a piece off the bottom of his blue and white striped galabia. "I don't like this thing anyway," he said as he bandaged Ben-Seyad's arm.

"We'd better go tell your grandpa what's going on," Ali said. "He's probably wondering where we are."

They climbed down the ladder and hurried to room 604. The door was unlocked. Don tapped several times, and when there was no answer, they went in. The three stood beside the bed where Grandpa lay, and Don whispered, "Grandpa Pete?"

His grandfather shot up. "What! Where—oh, Don, it's you," he said as if he'd forgotten where he was. Then he got a look at Ben-Seyad, standing next to Don. He sighed, lay back down, and closed his eyes. "I think I took too much medicine. I'm seeing double."

Don laughed and shook his grandfather to wake him up. "No, you're not, Grandpa Pete. This is Ben-Seyad. He's run away, and we have to hide him."

"Wait a minute. Wait a minute! Run away from whom?" Grandpa Pete kept staring from Don to his twin. "I can't believe what I'm seeing!"

"He ran away from an old creep named Abdul-Habib," Don said. "The guy was going to try to sell Ben-Seyad to Mom and Dad."

"Sell?" asked Grandpa. Ben-Seyad told Grandpa Pete about his life with Abdul.

After hearing Ben-Seyad's story, Grandpa Pete shook his head. "That's unbelievable! We knew Don had a twin, but I never thought we'd find you." Then he frowned. "We'll hide Ben tonight, but tomorrow we have to go to the authorities."

Ben-Seyad backed away. "You will send me to prison?"

"No, of course not," Grandpa Pete said. "We have to find out how we can make you a part of our family."

Ben-Seyad looked about ready to cry. Then he said softly, "I have never had a real family."

After they talked some more, Grandpa Pete said finally, "We can talk more tomorrow. You boys might want to go up on the roof to sleep tonight. It's cooler up there. And safer."

"Grandpa Pete, sir," Ali said. "Abdul was in the alley. He knows Ben-Seyad was coming here."

"I'll warn the night clerk that someone might be looking for you. He can send anybody who asks about you to my room. I'll take care of this Mister Abdul-Habib."

"Wait, before we go up to the roof, let me take a picture of you three with my new camera," Ali said. Don laughed at how excited Ali was about the camera.

Ben-Seyad, Don, and his grandfather stood with their arms around each other's waists. Ali took the picture. The photo came out of the camera, and they waited for the picture to appear. When he saw it, Don laughed. "You've cut off all our heads. You're a great photographer, Ali," he said, poking him on the arm. They all laughed.

Ali took two more pictures, but they were almost as bad. "I guess I need some practice."

"But not tonight," Grandpa Pete told him. "You boys get up to bed. We have a lot to do tomorrow."

Ali got extra straw mats and blankets and they returned to the roof. The chickens, aroused from their sleep, gave a few half-hearted squawks. Ali and his grandfather had a small shack in one corner of the roof, but the three boys spread their mats under the stars.

"Are you sleepy?" Don asked his twin as they all looked up into the huge sky.

"No. Just a little tired. So much has happened today." Ben-Seyad kept looking around, as if still afraid that Abdul would find him.

"Don't worry," Ali told him. "The only way to the roof is up the ladder from the top floor. I don't think that old man can jump from the next building."

"You don't know him," said Ben-Seyad. "He will keep trying to get me. He has terrible friends who will help him. He thinks I am worth money to him."

While Ben-Seyad was talking, Don was twisting the chain of the medallion. The moonlight glistened on the cobra.

Ben-Seyad leaned closer. "What is that you are wearing?" he asked.

"It's a royal medallion."

"May I see it?" Ben-Seyad asked.

"Sure. But be careful. I think it has special powers, at least for me. I look into the Eye of Horus, and everything goes black. I can see things happening in the past."

"It was pretty scary last time Dono looked

into the medallion," Ali said. "It was like he was in a trance or something. I was afraid his mind might get stuck back there in the past."

Don handed the medallion to his brother. Ben-Seyad rubbed his finger over the medallion and gasped. "It is hot." He dropped it onto his lap. "It is evil!"

"No, I don't think it's evil," Don said. "I know it sounds crazy, but I think it affects the two of us that way because we're related to royalty."

"You think we're related to the mummy your parents found?"

"No," explained Don. "That mummy was named Cobra. But he had a twin named Falcon. When their father the pharaoh died, Falcon was supposed to take over the throne because he was a few minutes older than Cobra.

"Cobra was jealous of his brother. They got into a fight, and Cobra thought he had killed his twin. He switched his Cobra medallion for the Falcon medallion and returned to the palace as Falcon. The Pharaoh's vizier was next in line after the twins. He thought one was dead, so he tried to kill the other."

"How do you know all this?" Ben-Seyad asked.

"I saw it all in the medallion. Then I learned

that Falcon didn't die in the fight. Falcon wrote a scroll telling what really happened. He put the scroll in a box with the Cobra medallion. It stayed hidden all these centuries."

"But why do you think we are descended from Falcon?"

"Because we look exactly like him. It was really weird. When I looked into the medallion, it was almost like I *was* Falcon. I could understand their language. I even knew what Falcon was thinking."

Ben-Seyad was quiet for a while. Then he picked up the medallion again. "I think Abdul discovered a secret tunnel and treasure that he's never told anyone about. He used to leave and be gone for a long time. And when he would return to the village, he would have money."

Don gave his twin a long look. "Are you thinking you might be able to see the treasure room in the medallion?"

Ben-Seyad nodded.

"Try to imagine the tomb," Don said. "Think about the guy buried there. What was he—a priest—vizier?"

"Yes. His name was Ahmeket. That's all I know about him. No, there is one other thing. He believed he had everlasting life."

"But all the ancient Egyptians thought that," Don said.

"He didn't just believe his soul would live forever in the other world. He thought he would live forever in *this* world."

As Ben-Seyad started to look into the Eye of Horus, Ali spoke up. "I don't think you should do this," he said. "We don't know enough about the power of the medallion. It could be dangerous."

"I am not afraid." But Ben-Seyad's hands shook a little as he concentrated on the Eye. He swayed, and then he put out his hands as if he were falling. Don remembered the scary feeling.

Ben-Seyad's breathing slowed, and he seemed relaxed now. "Can you hear me?" Don asked.

His brother nodded.

"What do you see?" Ali asked.

"I—I'm in a huge chamber—stone walls—it's like a laboratory. But it is also full of treasure and gold." He ducked down as if hiding from someone.

"I see a man in a yellow robe. He is wearing a medallion with a scarab beetle on it. He is mixing something in a green bowl shaped like a scarab. Now he has stopped to write something on a scroll."

Ben-Seyad gasped. "Someone else has come into the room. He looks like me!"

"It must be Falcon," Don whispered. "Ali, I'm going to try to look into the medallion, too. Maybe my brother and I can see the same thing."

"Please, don't, Dono."

"I have to. If that is Falcon, I have to know what happened to him."

Don moved closer to his brother, took his hand, and stared into the medallion. He felt the familiar sensation of falling, of a hot wind swirling around him like the beating of many wings....

The whirling stopped, and he could see what was happening in the past. He saw the chamber that Ben-Seyad had described. The man working at a stone table had his back to Don. In a green bowl shaped like a scarab, a liquid was boiling, sending wisps of steam into the air. Then Don saw a man in beggar's clothing and recognized Falcon.

Falcon stepped forward and said, "Well, Ahmeket, I have found you at last."

The other man whirled around. Don had seen him in the medallion before. He was the vizier who had killed Prince Cobra. He was holding a vial filled with a smoking liquid up to his lips. He drank some of it, and then saw

Falcon. A look of horror crossed his face, and he dropped the vial. "Cobra!"

"Not Cobra. I am Falcon," he said to the vizier. "Cobra left me for dead. But as you can see, I am alive."

Falcon looked around at the treasure. "I see you have already prepared for your death."

The vizier's smile was evil. "These treasures are not for the other world, Falcon." He nodded toward the green scarab bowl. "This potion will give me everlasting life."

Falcon moved toward the table. The vizier edged back. "What do you want, Falcon?"

"I want my rightful place as pharaoh of all of Egypt." As Falcon spoke, he moved steadily forward.

"The people think you are dead. You can never be pharaoh now. My son will be pharoah after me." The vizier picked up a gold statue and threw it at Falcon. It hit him in the face. But Falcon kept moving forward as if nothing could stop him.

His face twisted with rage, the vizier lunged at Falcon. The two struggled. Falcon pushed him away, and the vizier fell, hitting his head hard against the stone table. As he fell, the vizier's hand reached out to grab the green scarab bowl. It fell and crashed onto the stone floor. The liquid hissed and a cloud of fumes filled the room.

As if through a fog, Don saw Falcon pick up the lifeless vizier and carry him through an opening to a tunnel. He carried him to another chamber, and placed him in a coffin. Don saw the lid slam closed over the vizier.

"Dono! Ben-Seyad! Come back."

Faintly, Don heard Ali's voice. Then he felt someone shaking him. He slowly opened his eyes to see Ali kneeling beside him. "Are you all right, Dono?"

Don rubbed his forehead. "I'm okay." He looked at his twin who was opening his eyes.

"I have never had such a dream," Ben-Seyad said.

"That was no dream. It was the magic of the medallion," Don said. "You saw Falcon accidentally kill the vizier, didn't you?"

"How—how did you know?"

"Because I was watching the same thing. I don't think it's a dream. I think it really did happen a long time ago. That's the same vizier I saw before. He's the one who killed Cobra." Don shuddered.

"I wonder what he was drinking?" Ben-Seyad said.

"Whatever it was, he never got to finish it," Don answered.

"You two should never look into the Sacred

Eye again," Ali said. "When you were in that trance, neither one of you answered my questions. I was scared."

Ben-Seyad looked at Don and Ali. "I am sure now that Abdul found the vizier's chamber. That must be how he is getting money. He is still robbing from that chamber now."

"Tomorrow we can report it to the police," Don said. "But right now, I'm beat."

The three of them settled down on the mats. Ben-Seyad fell asleep first, with the medallion still around his neck. Don reached out to touch his brother's hand. "I'm glad we found each other, Ben," he said, leaving off the last part of the name. "Don't worry, we'll find a way to adopt you, too."

Don was asleep almost as soon as his head touched the mat. But instead of his usual nightmares about mummies, Don dreamed that he was introducing Ben to his friends at school.

He awakened slowly, feeling a little sick. Bright sunlight burned his eyes. A smell like strong medicine made him sick to his stomach. In a panic, he raised up and looked toward his brother's mat.

Ben was gone!

CHAPTER 5

In the Valley of the Kings

"ALI! Wake up! Ben's gone!"

Ali sat up looking around groggily. "Oooh, I feel awful," he moaned. "What's that smell?"

"I don't know," answered Don. "But I'm sure it has something to do with Ben's disappearance. Come on, let's go get Grandpa Pete!"

Don took off, stumbling down the ladder to the top floor. Ali was right behind him. They raced to room 604 and found the door partly open.

As Don started to go in, Ali whispered, "Dono, watch out. Somebody might be inside."

Carefully, Don pushed the door open wider until he could see his grandfather slumped in a chair. His head hung forward on his chest. That same smell was strong in the room. Don rushed forward.

"Grandpa Pete!"

His grandfather slid from the chair onto the floor. "He's dead!" Don cried. "Abdul killed him!"

As Don knelt beside his grandfather, Ali opened the window. "The smell is a lot stronger in here."

Then Don saw that his grandfather's chest was slowly moving up and down. "He's alive!" Don shook his shoulders. "Grandpa! Grandpa Pete!"

His grandfather groaned. "Stop yelling," he said feebly. "My head is exploding."

Don helped him sit up. "Ali, get a doctor."

"No, no," Grandpa Pete said. "I'll be fine in a minute. But how did anybody get in here? The door was locked."

"I'm going down to the desk and talk to the night clerk," Ali said. "I'll be right back."

"Grandpa, Abdul got Ben-Seyad!" cried Don. "I told him he'd be safe here. He trusted us, and now he's gone."

"I'm sorry, Don," Grandpa Pete said. "Abdul must be a pretty clever man to get past all of us."

"And what's that smell? Did he use some drug to knock us all out?"

Grandpa picked up a rag that smelled strongly. "Have you ever heard of chloroform?" he asked. "It knocks you out and gives you a nasty headache." He threw the rag out the window into the alley.

"I just got to know Ben a little," Don said, his voice choking. "And now he's gone."

Ali came rushing into the room. "Mustapha was still unconscious at the desk," he said. "Abdul must have knocked him out with that stuff and stolen a master key. I found this note on the desk, Grandpa Hunt. It's addressed to you."

Grandpa Pete opened the envelope. "It's in Arabic." As he read, his face turned red from anger. "It's from Abdul. He wants a million dollars for the boy. He says for us to go to Luxor and take a room at the New Winter Palace Hotel. He'll contact us in a few days to exchange the money for the boy."

"He must be crazy," Don said. "Where would we get a million dollars?"

Grandpa Pete shook his head. "I don't know. Abdul probably thinks all Americans are rich. The first thing we can do, though, is go to the bazaar and see what we can find out."

"Let me do that," Ali said. "People are more likely to talk to me."

"You're right," Grandpa said. "I'll tell the hotel that you're going to be our guide for the next few days. And I'll talk to your father, Ali. I think they'll let you go with us."

"All right!" Ali said. "I'll hurry right back."

"I'm going to lie down for a minute," Grandpa Pete said. "I'm feeling a bit shaky from that chloroform."

"I'll pack our bags," Don said. "Anything else, Grandpa Pete?"

"Get the desk clerk to make plane reservations for Luxor. And don't worry, Don. We'll find Ben-Seyad."

* * * * *

The next morning they arrived in Luxor. As soon as they were settled in the hotel, they went down to the desk to telephone Don's parents. The phone rang and rang at the other end, until someone picked it up.

"Mom! Dad!" Don yelled into the phone. "We found him!"

"You don't have to yell. We can hear you, son," his father said. "We're in Thailand, not on Mars. Who did you find?"

"We found Ben! My twin brother!" Don said.

"Donovan, are you sure?"

"Yes! He looks exactly like me. And he was found near a cave in the Valley of the Kings. Except there's a big problem. He's been kidnapped!"

"You'd better let me explain," Grandpa Pete said to Don and held out his hand to grab the phone.

"Get here as fast as you can," Don said, and then turned the phone over to his grandfather.

Grandpa Pete explained to Don's parents everything that had happened. Don listened impatiently.

"No, I don't think Abdul will hurt the boy as long as he thinks he can get money," Grandpa Pete said.

Don thought with a sick feeling about the bruises on Ben's face. When he got back on the phone again, he asked, "We can adopt Ben as soon as we get him back, can't we?"

"Of course," his mother said. "For years we have hoped to find him."

"Oh, that's great!"

"And don't worry, Don," his mother said. "We'll do whatever we have to do to get him. And, honey, having another son won't change the way we love you."

Don told his parents how much he missed them. Then Grandpa Pete talked to them a little longer. After he hung up, he asked, "Anybody have any bright ideas?"

"Ben mentioned a village where he lived," Don said.

"Do you know the name of the village?" Grandpa Pete asked.

"No, but it's near the Valley of the Kings. Ben said grave robbers have lived there for years and years."

Grandpa nodded. "I know the village. Come on."

They loaded their backpacks with some food, water, and supplies and walked to the dock area. They crossed the Nile River on a boat packed with tourists and hired donkeys to ride to the village. The desert sun roasted them, and the hot sands almost blinded them. The village was over five miles from the Valley of the Kings. It clung to the slopes of the tall cliffs. To Don the place was all broken stones, rubble, and dust, without a spot of green anywhere.

Grandpa Pete tried to talk to several people in Arabic, but they just shook their heads. Most Egyptians Don had met were friendly, but these villagers looked at them with suspicion.

"It was stupid to come here," Grandpa Pete said finally. "Now these people will probably tell Abdul that we know where he lives. I guess we'll have to go back to the hotel and wait."

"Grandpa, Ben told us something else," Don said. "He said Abdul had been working on the opposite side of the mountain from where Mom and Dad found the mummy of Prince Cobra. Ali and I know how to find it—I think."

"That's right," added Ali. "I remember the mountain shaped like a pink crocodile from last time."

"What do you think, Grandpa?" asked Don. "I think I can find it again. Can we go look for it?"

"I think it's worth a try," he answered. But we'll have to go back to town. We're not going out in that desert without plenty of supplies."

They headed back to their hotel. At dawn the next morning they started out, carrying enough food for two days, and tools and supplies on an extra donkey.

They headed west beyond the Valley of the Kings. Don kept his eyes open for the crocodile-shaped mountain, but nothing looked the way he remembered it. There were so many mountains, and each valley looked just like the last one. By the time they stopped for lunch, Don was getting discouraged.

"I'm sorry, Grandpa," he said. "I thought I'd be able to find the mountain right away."

They searched for the rest of the afternoon. One time, Ali pointed out some large birds circling over them in the hot desert sky.

"They're vultures," Grandpa Pete said

grimly. "I have a feeling they're not the only ones watching us."

"What do you mean, Grandpa Hunt?" asked Ali.

"Just think about it. Abdul knows we're here. He probably knows this desert like the back of his hand. Believe me, boys, he's out there somewhere, just watching us. We'll have to be careful."

When it started to get dark and they still hadn't spotted the crocodile mountain, they set up camp. After a cold meal of dates and bread, they stretched out in their sleeping bags. Don lay on his back staring up at the stars that looked close enough to touch.

"Ben," he whispered, right before he dropped off to sleep. "Maybe, somehow, you can hear me. Don't worry, I promise we'll find you."

Don woke up feeling sick. That terrible smell of chloroform was strong! Where was he? What was happening?

He felt himself being dragged. His back was banging against the ground. He threw out his arms to brace himself and touched rough material. He realized then that he must be in some kind of bag. Abdul! The old man must have knocked him out with chloroform and stuffed him in a sack. He was being dragged across the rocks and sand!

Don screamed, but his voice was weak. The bumping stopped for a minute, and Don tried to scream again. "Grandpa! Help me!"

Don had no idea how long he had been unconscious. They could be miles from the camp. "Abdul! I know it's you. Let me out!"

No answer. The bumping began again. Don's body felt bruised and sore from his head to his feet. Then, his head hit a rock, and he passed out again.

Suddenly, the bouncing stopped. He heard a scream and the sound of material ripping. Fresh air, then a terrible stench filled the air. It was a smell Don could never forget—the hideous smell of death and decay.

The mummy! Don remembered what had happened the last time he was in Egypt.

The linen wrappings had come loose, and Don could see the mummy's evil eyes and smell the dank mold. It was wearing a medallion.

Sweat soaked Don's shirt. He wanted to run but his feet wouldn't move. An overpowering force seemed to hold him. The mummy limped toward him. Don tried to scream, but the only sound that came from his paralyzed throat was a whistling gasp.

It came closer. And closer. Don felt its

breath. It smelled of death. Its shriveled black fingers closed about Don's wrist and clamped tight.

Don struggled, but the creature had the strength of a demon. The mummy picked him up as if he were a baby. Shuddering, half sick from the smell, Don tried to make himself a dead weight.

Then all was black again.

When Don awakened, every inch of his body ached. Then he remembered, and he screamed.

"Don! What's wrong?" Grandpa yelled and turned on his flashlight.

Don saw his grandfather and Ali. He was back in camp. Had he ever left it? Was it all a hideous dream? But he knew no dream could have made him ache all over. No dream smelled of chloroform—or of that other ghastly stench.

Don jumped up and groaned. "I don't know what happened. I thought Abdul had kidnapped me and dragged me away from camp. Then I think I dreamed the mummy picked me up and carried me back here." He shook his head. "I'm so confused. I—I don't know what really happened."

Ali was examining the area around the camp with his flashlight. "Look, Grandpa Hunt. It looks like something was dragged."

Don went over to look at the tracks. "I knew I wasn't dreaming. This proves that I was grabbed and taken away. I bet Abdul was trying to kidnap me, too. He probably thought he could get twice as much money for Ben and me both."

"But how did you get back here?" Ali asked. "Did you walk in your sleep?"

"The mummy...," said Don. "It was the mummy."

"Don, you had another one of your nightmares," his grandfather said.

"I thought so, too." Don sniffed his clothes. "But, Grandpa, smell this. It's the mummy."

His grandfather took a sniff of Don's shirt. "All I smell is chloroform. I know you weren't dreaming about that."

Don shook his head. "I don't know what to think. It seemed so real, but I guess it had to be a dream. I must have escaped and walked back here in a daze or something."

Grandpa Pete built a camp fire, and they sat up until it was light enough to travel again. They followed the path of drag marks for a short time, but it became difficult to follow because the wind had wiped out the tracks.

At midday, when they were about to give up and return to their hotel, Ali shouted,

"Look over there! Isn't that where we dug for water the last time we were here?"

Don slid off his donkey and ran over to Ali. "It sure looks like it. And this is where we first saw the pink mountain." Don looked toward the west. "There it is! I knew we could find it! Let's go!"

As their donkeys plodded over the rocky ground, the sun beat down on Don, Ali, and Grandpa Pete. Heat waves danced in front of their eyes. It was hard to breathe.

Late in the afternoon, they finally found the place where Don's parents had found the mummy. One side of the mountain had been destroyed when a supply of terrorist weapons blew up deep inside the mountain. They made their way to the other side. Sheer cliffs and an unbroken rock wall faced them.

Don's heart sank. "This doesn't look as if it's ever been used as a tomb," Don said.

Grandpa Pete slid off the donkey, and pointed to a crevice high up on the mountain. "The ancient tomb makers often used natural cuts in the mountain to start their tunnels."

"But I don't see any signs that Abdul has been digging here," Don said.

"Do you think he's going to leave a map for us?" Grandpa Pete asked. "We'll set up a camp nearby. You boys look for a gully where we can hide. If I'm right, and Abdul has been working in this spot, we don't want to let him know that we have found it."

As soon as they had hidden the donkeys, they began to search for an opening in the mountain. Except for the piles of broken rock, the place looked as if no one had been there for thousands of years. Grandpa Pete shook his head. "If Abdul and his grave-robber friends have worked here, they're certainly good at covering their tracks."

"I'm going to climb up to that crevice and take a look," Don said. He took one of the flashlights and started to climb. Don had spent his summers and vacations on archaeological digs with either his parents or his grandfather. He was a good climber. Using small footholds in the rock, Don made his way up the mountain.

"Do you see any signs of an opening?" called Grandpa Pete.

Don shined the light into the black hole. The rock looked solid. There was no sign of cuts with a chisel or pick.

"I can't see anything, Grand—no, wait!" He flashed the light over the back wall. "There's something white in there. I'm going in the hole."

"Be careful, Dono!" shouted Ali. "There might be snakes or scorpions in there—or worse."

Very carefully Don climbed into the crevice. Shining the light over the back wall, he saw something. He gave a cry and scrambled out of the crevice as fast as he could.

"Grandpa! Ali! Get up here quick!"

CHAPTER 6

The Mummy's Cruel Embrace

ALI and Grandpa Pete picked their way up the side of the mountain to the crevice. They climbed to where Don was standing. "What is it?" Grandpa Pete asked, out of breath.

Don held up a blood-soaked piece of blue and white cloth. "This is from my galabia. I think Ben left his bandage to show us how to find the opening to the tomb. It must be around here somewhere."

They shined their lights over the wall. "This looks like solid rock," Don said.

Grandpa Pete ran his hands over the rock. "I think we've found the entrance to the tomb, but it's been sealed up or hidden. Feel for cracks or anything different about the rock."

They carefully examined every inch of the solid wall. "It's no use," said Ali. "This stupid thing won't open." He kicked the stone wall near the bottom.

Suddenly, the stone wall began to rise.

"Ali!" shouted Don. "You found the spot!" The wall stopped moving when it was open only a foot or so. Don dropped to his knees and shined his light into the black hole. "I can't see anything, but I feel cold air. There must be a tunnel." He started to crawl under.

"Wait, Don," Grandpa warned. "The wall could drop right back down again."

They waited to see if the wall would drop back in place. "Abdul must have fixed the ancient door," Grandpa Pete said. "I think I underestimated him. That man is smart."

After a few minutes, Don said, "I've got to go in there. We have to find Ben."

Grandpa Pete said, "Okay, Don, go on in. But be careful. There's no telling what's inside. And try not to make any noise. If Abdul is in the tomb somewhere, we don't want to alert him."

Slowly, an inch at a time, Don squeezed under the door. He stood up on the other side of the door and shined his light all around. The walls were smooth, the work of the ancient tomb builders. He took a few steps forward, and then turned to call softly to Grandpa Pete. "It's a tunnel to a tomb, all right. Come on."

Don took a few careful steps ahead. Suddenly, his foot hit empty air, and he dropped his flashlight. He fell backward to keep from falling, too. It seemed like forever before it crashed somewhere far below. He lay there for a minute, panting for breath and hugging the flat rock floor. One more step and he would have joined his flashlight at the bottom of the hole.

"Be careful!" Don said as Ali and Grandpa Pete crawled into the tunnel. "There's a pit just ahead."

Ali shined his light down into the hole. The bottom far below was lined with sharp metal stakes. Don almost fainted. One more step and he would have felt the hideous stakes pierce his body.

Grandpa Pete put his arm on Don's shoulder. After a little while he said, "Feeling okay?"

Don nodded.

"The tomb builders sometimes dug a pit at the entrance, hoping to keep out grave robbers," Grandpa Pete explained. He ran his light on the side wall. "See that narrow ledge? Maybe there's another entrance over there."

"But how do we get to it?" Don asked.

"If there is another entrance, Abdul had to get to it," Grandpa said. "Don, go back to our supplies and bring me the hammer, the rope, and one of those spikes we brought along. I'll hammer the spike into the rock, attach the rope, and we can swing across to the ledge. Better bring the grappling iron, too. We might need it."

Don crawled back under the door, took several deep breaths of the fresh air, and then scrambled down the cliff. As he hurried to where they'd hidden the donkeys, he kept glancing at the sky. This was the first time he'd ever seen big dark clouds in Egypt. The sky was a sickly yellow-green, and storm clouds were moving in. He could hear thunder in the distance.

Don made sure that the animals and supplies were under an overhang of rock. Besides the things his grandfather wanted, Don found another flashlight, and filled his backpack with food and an extra canteen of water.

As he was loading up, he noticed a cloud of dust in the east. Was it Abdul and the grave robbers? Or was it just the wind making swirling dust devils? He couldn't tell.

He ran back to the tomb. Climbing back up to the entrance with his arms full, he slipped several times on the loose rubble. Before he reached the top, huge raindrops began to pelt him. Lightning zigzagged down from the sky and struck a mountain nearby. The skies seemed to open up, and rain slashed at his face.

"Hurry up, boy," his grandfather called from inside the tunnel. "It doesn't just rain cats and dogs in Egypt. It rains camels and crocodiles."

Ali ran out to give him a hand with the supplies. They were both soaked by the time they squeezed under the door to the tunnel.

"Grandpa! I saw a cloud of dust to the east of us. I think someone might be following us."

Grandpa Pete looked worried. "Those villagers probably warned Abdul and his friends that we were looking for him," he said. "We'd better hurry and find the entrance to the tomb."

He took the spike and hammered it into the solid rock, and then attached a rope to it. "I'll go first," he said. "If I don't make it across, you boys hightail it back to town."

Don held his breath as his grandfather swung out over the deep black pit. His feet missed the ledge, and he had to start over. After several tries he made it across. "You two wait until I see if I can find an entrance," he said.

Grandpa Pete moved along the narrow ledge until he was out of sight. In a little while, the boys heard his voice. “I’ve found the entrance. Come on across.”

Ali swung safely over. As Don swung over the pit, he tried not to think about the horrible stakes below. When Don reached the entrance, Grandpa Pete and Ali had already started down the steep steps of the tunnel. In several places, the tunnel was full of rubble.

“The terrorists’ explosion last time must have damaged this tomb,” Grandpa Pete said.

Finally they came to a large chamber, empty except for a few pieces of broken furniture. “Looks like robbers stripped all the gold treasure from this room a long time ago,” Grandpa said. Don and Ali were looking at the painted walls. “Those are scenes from the Book of the Dead, which the ancient Egyptians used to prepare bodies for the afterlife,” Grandpa said. “But we can’t waste time sightseeing, boys. Let’s go.”

They followed a long tunnel into another chamber. “Look up there,” said Grandpa Pete. The roof had caved in. There was light coming in from a small opening high above them. Don put his flashlight in his pack and looked around.

This room was empty too, except for a few pieces of furniture, clothing, and weapons. Grandpa Pete pointed to a table that was covered with dried up food. "That's for mummies to eat in the next world," he said.

Ali looked at the food on the plates. "Blecchh!" he said. "Good thing I'm not hungry."

Don poked him on the arm. "Hey, didn't you hear Grandpa Pete? It's not for you anyway," he said with a laugh. "It's mummy food."

Chunks of rock and rubble lay everywhere. "We must be deep inside the mountain," Grandpa said. "When the terrorists' supplies blew up on the other side of the mountain, it must have wrecked part of this tomb, too."

Don was examining the walls. "I don't see any way into the next chamber or tunnel."

"There has to be one that leads to the burial room," Grandpa said.

"It could take hours to check every inch of this chamber," Don said. "We'll never find Ben."

"Look over here, Dono." Ali pointed to a red spot on the wall. "I thought it was part of the wall painting, but I think it's blood."

Don touched the spot. "I think you're right, Ali. It is blood. But what does it mean?"

"Maybe it's a sign from Ben-Seyad that we should look on this wall," Ali said.

"Hmm, maybe you're right," answered Don.

He noticed a large box, about seven feet long in a corner of the chamber. "Ali, help me pull this thing over to the wall. I want to try to reach the ceiling here."

Tugging and pulling, they moved the box and leaned it up against the wall. When Don climbed up on it, he could almost reach the ceiling. As he began feeling along the wall for a crack, he heard a snap. Suddenly, one foot went through the rotted wood. With a crash of splintering wood, the whole box caved in, and Don fell into it.

There was something in the box—something revolting and hateful. Don looked around him and gagged. He was in the grotesque embrace of two unwrapped mummies. Blackened, shriveled arms and legs surrounded him. The hideous head of one seemed to be grinning at him.

"Arrghh! Help!" he shrieked hysterically. "Get me out of here!"

As he tried to claw his way out, he kept slipping. Ali was finally able to help him out, and Don tried not to be sick. Don sat in a corner, his eyes closed, trying to get rid of the sight of the mummies' grinning faces and the horrible feel of their hands on his body.

"Shhh, listen!" Grandpa said. "Do you hear that?"

Don sat still, holding his breath. "Sounds like water."

"I hope I'm wrong," Grandpa said, "but I'm afraid..."

A thundering roar cut him off as a torrent of water crashed into the chamber from the hole in the roof. The force of the water knocked Don over, and he crashed into the back wall. Stunned for a second, his head went under water. He fought his way to the surface, coughing and gasping for breath. The sound of the water's roar was deafening.

He looked around for his grandfather and Ali. Grandpa Pete was thrashing at the water. "Are you okay?" Don yelled to him over the roar.

"Yeah. All this water is from the rainstorm over the mountain! Where's Ali?"

Ali's head burst up from the churning, swirling water that was quickly filling the chamber. "Help!" He yelled as his head went under again.

Don saw a box floating nearby. He grabbed it and swam toward where his friend had disappeared.

Ali surfaced again. "Can't swim," he said, choking.

"Hold onto this box!" Don shouted. "It will float." Don helped Ali reach the box.

They treaded water for what seemed like hours. Finally, the water stopped thundering through the hole in the ceiling, and it slowed to a steady stream.

Don held his flashlight above his head and shined it upwards. With horror, he realized that they were floating only a foot or so from the ceiling. And the water was still coming in!

"Grandpa Pete!" he shouted. "What do we do if the room fills clear to the top? We won't be able to breathe!"

Suddenly something floated near Don's face. "Aaarrgh!" he yelled as one of the mummy's hands brushed against his face. With a shudder, he splashed it away. He watched as it slowly sank below the surface.

Now the water level was less than a foot from the ceiling. If it rose any higher, there wouldn't be enough room to breathe. Panic overcame Don. He felt the water tugging him down. Or was it the mummy's hand?

He looked over toward Ali. Their eyes met. Ali's eyes looked like those of a frightened animal.

"Grandpa!" Don cried. "We're going to die!"

CHAPTER 7

Trapped!

"THE water has almost stopped coming through the hole," Grandpa Pete said. "The rainstorm must be over. I think we'll be all right."

Don took a deep breath. He told himself that his grandfather had been in plenty of tough spots before. If he thought they would be okay, that was good enough for Don.

"We have to work fast before the water level drops," Grandpa Pete said, pointing to the jagged hole in the ceiling where the water had rushed through. "Don, climb up there and try to see what's on the other side of this wall."

Don reached up and grabbed at a jagged edge of stone. His fingers slipped, and he fell back. His head went under water. He came up gasping for breath.

"Let me try it," Ali said. "I have strong arms from carrying heavy suitcases." Ali pulled himself up to the opening.

"What do you see?" Grandpa Pete asked. "Can we get to the outside?"

Ali shook his head. "No, the hole where the water broke through is too high to reach. But there's a room on the other side of this chamber. If we can break loose some more rock, I think we can get into it."

"Don, get the chisel and rope out of my pack," Grandpa said, pointing over his shoulder.

Treading water, Don searched through his grandfather's backpack. "It's a good thing we put those plastic bags around all the stuff, Grandpa," said Don. "We thought it would keep out the sand. Now it's keeping out this water!"

He pulled out the chisel and rope and handed them to his grandfather.

"Ali, take the rope and tie one end around your waist," Grandpa Pete said. "Then see if you can hook the other end around that rock that's sticking out." As he talked, he was pulling himself up to the opening.

"You're right, Ali," he said. "Only a little water has splashed over into the chamber. If I can make this hole wider, we've got it made."

Grandpa Pete began chipping away at the wall. It crumbled easily. He chipped at the rock for a while, and then said, "We're going to have to drop down into the chamber on our ropes."

Ali went first. "Are you okay?" Don called when he heard Ali hit the floor.

"Wow! You should see this place. I think we've found the burial room!" Don could hear the excitement in Ali's voice. Don went next. The wet rope stung his cold hands as he slid down. His grandfather was right behind him.

They stood and gaped at the burial room. Light from the small opening in the ceiling gleamed on the gold treasures—statues, chests, couches, even a gold chariot. The walls were covered with colorful hieroglyphics. In the middle of the large chamber sat the open stone sarcophagus. And inside it was a coffin.

Grandpa Pete let out his breath in a whistle. "It doesn't look as if our friend Abdul has had a chance to rob this grave room yet. The tomb builder really hid it well." Then Grandpa Pete saw the look on Don's face and said, "Don, what's wrong?"

Grandpa Pete and Ali looked at Don. He was pale and had a frightened look on his face.

"This is unbelievable," Don said slowly. "I—I know you're not going to believe me, but I've seen this room before."

"That's impossible," said Grandpa. "When could you have seen this room?"

"I saw it when I looked into the medallion," Don said. "I saw Falcon bring the dead vizier down a tunnel to this room and put Ahmeket in this coffin." Don shivered.

Grandpa Pete sighed. "I wish you'd forget this medallion business."

"I can't forget it, Grandpa."

"I hate to bring this up," Ali said, "but how do we get out of here? It might take weeks for the water to seep out of that other chamber."

"Listen, let me see if I can remember what I saw in the medallion," said Don. "Falcon came down a tunnel. The door was open to this room, but I can't remember where it was exactly. It was on this wall, I think."

"Don, I told you. That was a dream."

"It was not, Grandpa. I know it wasn't." Then he told his grandfather everything he had seen in the medallion.

"All right," Grandpa Pete said after he had heard the story. "Let me take a look at this wonderful magic medallion."

"Uh, I don't have it," Don answered. "Ben's got it. But I wish I did have it. Then maybe it would help us get out of here."

Grandpa Pete just shook his head.

* * * * *

Before it got dark in the tomb, they took the things out of their packs. Thanks to the plastic bags, the food was only a little bit soggy. They spread their clothes out to dry. Ali actually got a good picture of the coffin with his new camera. They found dry places to sit and ate some food.

After a while, the three of them were yawning. "I'm so tired, I could sleep on top of the coffin," Grandpa said. "How about you boys?"

"Anywhere but there," Ali said. Don and Ali made themselves comfortable on wooden couches, while Grandpa Pete stretched out on the coffin. Don wasn't exactly scared, but he felt uneasy in the burial room. The pale light of the moon coming through the hole in the top of the mountain turned everything to a ghostly silver. Finally he drifted off to sleep.

Don could hear his own footsteps in the silent street. He couldn't remember Cairo ever being so quiet. The palm trees cast strange shadows, and the streetlights looked like pale, dead moons.

He heard a padding sound behind him. Sliiiip-thud, sliiiip-thud, like someone or something dragging one foot. For a second, he froze. And then he felt a burning at the back of his neck, and he began to run.

Sliiiip-thud, faster and faster behind him...

Don shot up from the couch he was sleeping on. He was drenched with sweat. Would he ever stop dreaming about the mummy?

He lay for a long time shivering, even though the burial room was warm. His grandfather reached out a hand and took Don's. "It's all right, Don. You're safe with me."

"Thanks, Grandpa," Don whispered. "I'm okay now." He fell asleep again and had no more nightmares.

When Don woke up, he found Ali already searching the walls for a hidden door. "Look," Ali whispered, trying not to wake up Grandpa.

"What are you two whispering about? Grandpa asked. "Are you afraid you'll wake the mummy?"

The boys grinned. In the daylight, the burial room didn't seem so scary. Ali pointed to the wall that Don had seen in the medallion. "The design on this wall is different from the others," he said.

"Hmm, you're right," said Grandpa Pete, coming over to look at it. They started tapping on the wall. Where the design was different, the wall gave off a hollow sound.

"I think there's another room or a tunnel

here," Ali said. As he spoke, he pressed a place on the wall. Suddenly, the wall began to tilt outward like a garage door opening.

Grandpa Pete shone his flashlight into the darkness. "It looks like a tunnel. Let's see where it leads."

"It goes to a scientist's laboratory," Don muttered.

Grandpa Pete turned around. "I suppose you know that from the magic medallion, too."

Don said nothing. He only looked at Ali.

Cautiously moving forward, they made their way along the passageway. After a while, they came to a place where another tunnel took off in a different direction.

"If I'm not all turned around," Grandpa Pete began, "I think this other tunnel will lead us back to where we started. We should be able to find our way out."

"But what about Ben?" Don asked. "He has to be in here somewhere."

"You boys go back to the burial chamber, and eat your breakfast. You can wait there while I go find the way out of here. I'll come back with some more water and supplies. And don't worry, Don. We won't leave without finding Ben. Just promise you won't go hunting for him without me."

Don and Ali promised and returned to the

burial room, while Grandpa Pete headed down the other tunnel. While they finished eating the food they had brought, Don looked around the burial room. The boys soon got tired of waiting and started to examine some of the treasures in the room. "Wow," Ali said. "I'll bet there's more stuff here than they found in King Tut's tomb."

"It's really weird," Don said, his voice shaking slightly, "but when I looked in the medallion back in Cairo, I actually saw Falcon put the vizier in that coffin."

"The vizier? Wasn't he the guy who was going to live forever in this world," Ali whispered. "Do you—" He swallowed hard. "Do you think he's really in the coffin, or—or is he walking around in these tunnels?"

Don shot him a quick look. "You don't really believe he could do that, live forever and walk around in the tomb, do you? He's been dead for 5000 years. Come on, Ali. You're the one with the scientific mind."

"No, I guess I don't believe it," Ali said, sounding doubtful. "But like your grandpa said, strange things can happen."

"Wait a minute! What am I talking about?" Don cried. "There can't be a mummy in the coffin. Falcon put the vizier right in the coffin, and he wasn't embalmed and wrapped in bandages or anything. The only thing in the coffin is a skeleton—or a pile of dust!"

"Yeah, I guess that's right," Ali said. "Who's afraid of a pile of bones?"

They sat for a while staring at the coffin, until Don said, "Hey Ali, you know what? The vizier was wearing a medallion that looked like the Cobra and Falcon ones. Maybe if we open the coffin and get the medallion, I could see into it and find out how to get to that room. Maybe it'll help us find Ben."

Ali looked nervous. "I don't know. Maybe we should just leave it alone until your grandfather gets back."

"But, Ali, you know what he thinks about the medallion. He wouldn't let us open the lid to get the medallion because he doesn't think it can do all the stuff I said it can."

"I still don't think it's a good idea," Ali said.

Don looked serious. "What if it's the only way to find Ben? You know he's somewhere around here. How would you feel if we didn't do everything we could to find him? I know how I'd feel." Then he added, "And don't forget, Ali. Ben is my brother."

Ali stared at the coffin. Then he looked back at Don. "All right," he said softly. "I'll do it for you—and Ben."

Don stood up and walked slowly over to the

coffin. Now that he had decided to open it, he felt afraid. Ali stood right behind him. Don's hand was shaking as he reached out to lift the heavy lid.

"Don!"

Don jumped a foot. "Ali, you scared the daylights out of me! What's wrong?"

"Leave it alone until your grandpa comes back."

"We have to get the medallion," Don said. "We may never see Ben again if we don't open the lid. Besides, it's not a mummy, it's just a dusty old skeleton. A skeleton can't hurt us."

"Well, what if there's a curse on it like on the Cobra mummy?" Ali pleaded.

Don hesitated. He remembered the mummy's curse—*Whoever touches me or my treasure is doomed for eternity.* "Well," he said, "I've already slept on his couch. If there's a curse, we're already doomed."

Taking a deep breath, Don turned back around and looked at the coffin. It took all his strength to lift the heavy lid. He closed his eyes and opened the lid.

When he heard Ali scream in terror, Don opened his eyes and looked into the coffin. There, grinning up at him with hideous yellow teeth and blackened lips, was the most horrible thing he had ever seen.

CHAPTER 8
It's Alive!

LYING in the coffin was a revolting, blackened, shriveled shape that barely looked like it had once been human. Don and Ali gazed in utter horror at the hideous teeth and lips smiling up at them, the rotted hole where the nose should be, the leathery eyelids that were closed, and the long thin hands crossed over the chest.

Don yelled and jumped back in fright. As he did, liquid from a small bottle attached to the lid of the coffin spilled onto the ghastly face.

And then the evil yellow eyes opened and stared up at them. The ghastly teeth and lips moved. The thin hands twitched. And the rotted hole of a nose began to breathe. Slowly the blackened thing raised up in the coffin. Don shrieked and slammed down the lid.

"Ali! It's alive! Run!"

His breath coming in great gasps, Don raced out of the burial room into the pitch black tunnel. Ali was right behind him. He bumped into Don, and they both shrieked in terror. They wanted to run. But without flashlights, they had to feel their way along slowly.

"Grandpa!" Don shouted hysterically. "Grandpa, where are you?"

"Shhh!" Ali hissed. "That—that thing will know where we are. Get a hold of yourself, Dono," Ali added. "We've got to stay cool."

"Yeah, you're right. But I really flipped out when I saw that thing!"

Silently, they groped their way along the tunnel a while longer until they came to the place where two tunnels went in different directions. They took the one they hoped would lead out of the tomb. But soon they came to another split. They couldn't guess which direction to take.

"Listen!" Don stopped dead in his tracks. "Do you hear that? Coming from the tunnel to the right?"

"Hear what?" Ali asked.

"It—it sounded like something walking slowly, dragging one foot, just like—just like the mummy! The one from the museum that came up the elevator at the hotel to get me. The one that disappeared from the museum!"

"I'll believe anything after seeing that thing rise up in the coffin," said Ali. "But what would the mummy from the museum be doing here?"

"I don't know, but I'll never forget that sound, Ali. Come on! Let's take the tunnel to the left and get away from it—whatever it is."

After what seemed like hours of creeping silently along the passageway, Don saw a faint light ahead around a bend in the tunnel. He stopped and whispered to Ali. "What do you think it is?"

"We can't be sure," Ali said. "It could be Abdul and his men. Or it could be your grandfather."

"Or we could be going in a circle, and it's that awful thing. What should we do, Ali? There's no place to hide."

Slowly, they backed up. The light grew brighter, and the footsteps came closer. "If it's only Abdul, we can handle him," Ali said. "He's old and small."

Don waited, his heart pounding so loud that it seemed to echo down the tunnel. When the light was almost on them, he tensed up, ready to jump the person who was coming.

"Get ready," he whispered in Ali's ear. "He's almost here!"

Together, Ali and Don yelled and leaped

on the figure with the light.

"Hey! Get off me!" yelled Grandpa Pete from under the pile of boys.

He saw who had jumped him and frowned. "What's going on? You boys almost gave me a heart attack. I told you to stay in the burial room."

"Grandpa, we saw...we saw..." Don gulped. "We have to get out of here now and get help."

"You saw Abdul?"

Don shook his head. "No! It wasn't Abdul, it was the v—v—vizier, Ahmeket," he stuttered.

"You boys *opened* that coffin?"

"Yes," Don said, talking a mile a minute. "The vizier was in it. Grandpa, he was hideous, all blackened and shriveled up. And when the coffin opened, it made a bottle of some kind of liquid spill on him. Then he—he opened his eyes and rose up." Don shuddered again.

Grandpa Pete laughed. "You boys just let your imaginations run away with you. Come on. We'll go back to the chamber."

"Grandpa, no! Don't go back there," Don pleaded. "Ali and I both saw it. It's alive!"

"Well, even if it is alive, if it's all shriveled up, it's no match for the three of us, is it?" Grandpa chuckled. "But you can wait outside the chamber. I'll show you there's no vizier walking around in there."

They started back to the burial room, Don and Ali following behind Grandpa Pete. When they came to the place where Don had thought he'd heard the footsteps, he stopped to listen.

Nothing.

Don hurried to catch up with the others, telling himself that maybe it had been his imagination after all.

Walking back to the burial room with the flashlight didn't seem to take nearly as long as their escape in the dark had seemed to take. They waited in the tunnel with the flashlight while Grandpa Pete went into the burial room. He called, "It's okay, boys. There's nothing in the coffin, no mummy, no skeleton—nothing."

Slowly, Don and Ali entered the room. "The vizier must have taken the other tunnel," Don said.

"Don, I can tell you're letting this place get to you," his grandfather said calmly. "But I'm surprised at *you*, Ali. You have a sensible head on your shoulders."

"Grandpa Hunt, sir, we did see it—just like Don said." Ali went over to the coffin and felt along the inside. "Look, see this bottle?

There's still some liquid in it. And feel the coffin. It's still wet."

Grandpa Pete felt the inside of the coffin. "Hmm. It must have gotten splashed with water when the rain came in. That's what must have happened."

Don shook his head. "I'm just not sure what to think anymore. This place is so creepy that you start to think anything could happen. Maybe you're right, Grandpa. Maybe it was just my imagination."

"Wait a minute!" Ali shouted. "The coffin wasn't open when the rain came in. It couldn't have gotten wet that way!"

Grandpa Pete gave Ali a funny look. Then he went over and felt the inside of the coffin again and scratched his head.

"How come you don't believe us, Grandpa Pete? You always say that strange things happen in this world that nobody can explain."

Grandpa Pete looked confused. "Well, that's right. I do say that sometimes. But I think there has to be an explanation for this."

"Maybe the vizier made a potion to keep him in suspended animation all these years," Don said.

"Yeah," Ali added, "and maybe he rigged the coffin so that when somebody opened it later, that liquid would spill on him and bring him back to life."

"You boys have been reading too many science-fiction stories," Grandpa Pete said. "I think a grave robber was in this room. When he heard us coming, he hid in the coffin. Imagine how scared *he* must have been when you opened the lid."

Don shook his head. "That wasn't any ordinary person in there."

"Well, as a matter of fact, I saw an ordinary person. I forgot about it when you guys jumped me. I saw Abdul. He was carrying a bag and was headed away from the tomb. He didn't see me."

"I'll bet he's hidden Ben in the vizier's secret laboratory," Don said.

"Don, I don't want to hear any more about secret laboratories," Grandpa Pete said. "Now, grab all our stuff, and come on. We have to find Ben."

They gathered up their supplies and headed down the tunnel that they hoped would take them to Ben. Soon the pitch black tunnel got smaller. They had to crawl on their hands and knees for a while.

Grandpa Pete was in the lead. Suddenly, he yelled and disappeared.

"Grandpa!" Don screamed.

Don crawled carefully forward and saw that his grandfather had fallen into another pit. "Are you all right?" Don called. But Grandpa Pete didn't answer. The only thing Don and Ali heard was a loud hissing sound.

Ali shined his flashlight into the pit. They saw Grandpa Pete lying on the ground. Near his head was a large snake.

Grandpa Pete groaned and rolled over.

"Don't move, Grandpa," called Don. "There's a snake in the pit. I'm coming down."

Don quickly tied the rope around his waist and had Ali tie the other end to a large rock.

"Hurry, Dono," said Ali. "We don't know how long that snake will stay away."

Don lowered himself the 10 feet down into the snake pit while Ali shined the light down.

"Roll slowly to your left, Grandpa," he said. "Are you hurt?"

"It's my ankle," he answered weakly. "I landed hard on it. I think it's broken."

Don lowered himself to the floor of the pit and moved very slowly toward his grandfather, trying not to make any sudden moves. He kept his eye on the snake, which was swaying from side to side and flicking out its tongue.

"Here's the rope, Grandpa. I'll tie it around your waist, and we'll try to lift you out. Use your good leg to help us."

With a groan of pain, Grandpa Pete slowly and carefully lifted himself up and over to the wall. Don stood between Grandpa Pete and the snake, using his backpack as a shield. Once when Grandpa Pete stumbled, the snake lashed out. Don knocked it away with his pack.

"Hurry, this snake is getting mad!"

With a lot of straining and groaning, Ali and Don finally got Grandpa Pete out of the snake pit. Ali threw the rope back down, and Don climbed up out of the pit.

"It's my ankle, boys," said Grandpa Pete, breathing hard. "It's swollen pretty badly."

After they rested for a time, Ali asked,

"How did the snake live in that pit for thousands of years?"

"It didn't," Grandpa said. "I bet Abdul and his friends put it there to keep out intruders. This tunnel must lead to something important, or there wouldn't be a pit or snakes here," Grandpa Pete said.

Grandpa Pete tried to stand on his ankle, but the pain was too great. He fell back down onto the hard stone floor of the tunnel.

"I can't walk," he said. "You'll have to go look for Ben without me."

"But we can't leave you here, Grandpa."

"You have to, Don. I'll be okay. You have

to come back this way, and you can help me out then. Take some of my supplies with you." Grandpa Pete winced in pain when he moved his ankle.

"But..." Don started to say.

"I know you and Ali can do it," Grandpa Pete reassured them.

"But..."

"Go! You've got to find him!"

CHAPTER 9

The Chamber of Horror

DON got the grappling hook from Grandpa Pete's pack, attached it to the rope, and tossed it to the other side of the pit. The hook caught in the hard-packed dirt and rock. Hand over hand, Don started along the rope across to the other side. His hands were sweaty, and it was hard not to let them slip off the rope. He could hear the hissing below him.

When he made it safely across, he whistled to Ali, who quickly made it across, too. They both called good-bye to Grandpa Pete and hurried on through the tunnel. The tunnel widened and was high enough for them to walk comfortably. As they walked, they talked quietly.

Don shined the light on his calendar watch. "It's been almost three days now since Abdul sent the message. What do you think he'll do to Ben if we aren't at the hotel with the money?"

"I think your grandpa's right. Abdul won't hurt Ben as long as he thinks he can sell him back to us. But I'm more worried about the vizier."

Just then an awful thought struck Don. "Ali! Ben and I look just like Prince Falcon. What if Ahmeket finds Ben and thinks he's Falcon?"

"I don't know, Dono," he answered. "But it doesn't sound too good."

"Let's hurry."

They had walked about five minutes more when suddenly they heard a loud metallic sound. Before they could react, two sets of heavy iron bars crashed to the floor of the tunnel behind and in front of them. They were trapped in a cage.

Don tugged at the bars. "We must have tripped a wire or something," he said. "There has to be some way to re-open this thing. Look around."

Using the flashlights, they examined the ground outside the cage. "There's dirt piled up on both sides of the cage," Ali said. "It goes almost all the way to the sides of the tunnel. Unless you knew it was there, you couldn't miss stepping on it."

"Maybe we can reach through the bars and

press on it to make the bars go up," Don said.

He lay on the ground and stretched his arm as far as he could. But his fingers couldn't reach the raised spot in the dirt.

"Toss one of our packs on it," Ali suggested. "Maybe it's heavy enough to trigger it."

They tossed both packs, but nothing happened.

"I'm pretty skinny," Ali said. "Maybe I can squeeze through the bars."

"You can try it, but they're awfully close together."

Ali took off his galabia, got on the ground, turned onto his side, and started to push his slender body through the bars. "I can almost make it, but not quite. I wish I had some grease or oil," he said. "Then I might be able to slide through."

"I'm sure we don't have anything like that in the packs, but I'll look."

Don looked through the packs. At the bottom of his pack, he found something he had forgotten he had brought along. "Hey, how about this?" he said holding up a bottle of insect repellent. "This stuff's a little greasy."

"Yeah," said Ali. "It might help me get through the bars and it'll keep the bugs off me!"

"Very funny," said Don as he began rubbing it on Ali's arms and legs and shoulders, and even on the bars. Squeezing and pushing, Ali finally wriggled through the bars. He got up and stood on the raised dirt on the ground.

Don held his breath. They heard a grinding sound, and the bars slowly raised up into place in the roof of the tunnel. Don gave a sigh of relief.

"How many more of these booby traps do you think there are?" Don asked.

"I don't know," Ali said. "But we have to be more careful."

"At least all these traps tell us that we're heading toward an important place," said Don. "Maybe it'll be the laboratory I saw in the medallion."

After another half an hour, they stopped for a rest. Walking in the hot cramped tunnels had made them very tired. They both just sat there, not saying anything for a while. Finally Don said, "Ali, do you think we'll ever find Ben and get out of this place?"

"All we can do is hope," said Ali thoughtfully, "and keep cool."

"Do you think it will be hard to get permission to take Ben out of the country?"

"I don't know. The police would never give Ben back to Abdul. And it should help that you and Ben are twins."

"I sure hope Mom and Dad are at the hotel when we get out of here," Don said. "Grandpa left word that we were here looking for Abdul. They'll go right to the police. Well," added Don, getting to his feet, "let's get going."

They started on again. They hadn't been walking for more than five minutes when the tunnel took a sharp turn to the right. Suddenly, they were at a dead end.

The wall looked solid, but now they knew that there had to be a way to open it. Don found the hidden lever, and the wall opened up.

They had to cover their eyes because of the light flooding out of the room from torches on the walls. Inside was a huge, almost empty chamber—the same room Don remembered from the medallion. The walls were covered by colorful hieroglyphics. But now the room was damaged. Bits of rock and sand kept falling through a huge crater in one wall.

"This place must have gotten wrecked by the terrorists' explosion," said Don as they started to explore. "But it's definitely the same room I saw in the medallion."

Ali pointed to some modern lab equipment in a corner, next to a wooden screen. "Abdul must be melting down the gold stuff here,"

Ali said. "Ben said that Abdul seemed to have money when no one else in the village did."

They walked slowly toward the equipment and the screen, all the while looking around them for signs of Abdul or the horrible vizier.

Don walked to the wooden screen. "Ali," he whispered, "there's something behind the screen."

"Be careful, Dono. You don't know what it is."

Taking a deep breath, Don looked behind it. There, lying still on a stone slab, was his brother Ben. His eyes were closed, and he was tied to the slab with leather thongs.

"Ben! Ben, we're here! We found you!"

But Ben didn't move.

"Oh, no! Ali, he's dead!" Don cried.

CHAPTER 10

Face to Face with Terror

ALI rushed over. He listened to Ben's heart and felt for a pulse at his neck. "I don't think he's dead, Dono. He feels warm," Ali said. "I think he's in a coma."

Don started to shake his brother, but he couldn't wake him from his coma. He untied the leather thongs that held him. "Ben! Ben! Wake up!" he shouted hysterically until Ali held his arm. "Do you think he'll come out of it?" he asked Ali with tears in his eyes.

"I don't know, Don," Ali answered. They slumped to the floor beside Ben's motionless body. Don buried his head in his arms and sobbed. Ali put his arm around him. They sat for a while in the flickering light of the torches in the silent tomb.

"Don, look at those jars there, by the table."

Don looked up and saw several small clay jars on the floor.

"Those are funerary jars. The ancient Egyptians used those to embalm mummies. They took out the lungs, liver, and stomach and put them in the jars."

Ali whistled.

"Are you thinking what I'm thinking?" asked Don.

Ali nodded.

Don said, "I know it sounds incredible, but I think the vizier is planning to embalm Ben."

"Why would he do that?" asked Ali.

"Maybe the vizier thinks that Ben is Cobra or Falcon because he looks just like them. Ahmeket would embalm a prince and make a mummy out of him."

"Dono, do you think the vizier and Abdul saw each other?"

"I don't know."

"And who tied Ben up and put him in the coma?"

"I know one thing," said Don. "The vizier would have been plenty mad if he found Abdul melting down his treasures. The vizier needed all those things for his everlasting life."

"Look," said Ali, reaching into one of the jars. "A scroll. It's so old it's about to fall apart."

"I remember that when I looked into the

medallion before, I saw the vizier writing on a scroll just before Falcon found him. Can you read it?" Don asked.

"I don't know," answered Ali. "It's written in hieroglyphics. I haven't studied this very much."

"You have to try, Ali!"

Ali studied it for a while. "It's tough to read. I can only make out a little of it. The vizier wrote it, all right. He's telling about a plan. He says he was very sick, so he made a potion that would put him in—he calls it something like the sleep of the living death."

"That sounds kind of like a coma, doesn't it?"

Ali nodded. "But it sure didn't work. He looked awful."

"In the medallion," explained Don, "I saw Falcon knock a bowl of some stuff out of the vizier's hand. He only drank part of it. Maybe it would have worked if he could have drunk all of it. What else does the scroll say?"

"Well, there's a bunch of stuff here I can't read—about Horus and other gods. Then he says he planned to drink the potion. And before it had time to work, he would climb into his coffin. He figured when he woke up again the cure for his illness would have been discovered."

"He rigged the coffin," Ali continued, "so that whenever the tomb was discovered, and someone opened the lid, a bottle of another potion would splash on him. And then he would wake up. There's more stuff here that I can't read at all."

"This is incredible," said Don. "Do you think the vizier mixed up some more of that potion and gave it to Ben?"

"Like you said, Dono—it's incredible. But I think that's what happened!"

"Then why wouldn't the other potion bring Ben back? There's some liquid left in that bottle in the coffin back in the burial room."

"But we could never get back there. It's too far and too dangerous."

"Yeah," said Don with disappointment. "If only we could find another tunnel, a shortcut."

Both boys were quiet again, feeling the helplessness of the situation. Then Don snapped his fingers. "Wait a minute! The medallion! Why didn't I think of that before?" He jumped up and took the medallion from around Ben's neck. "Maybe I can look into it and see how Falcon got to the burial room after he fought with the vizier. I just know there's another tunnel. There's got to be."

"Aren't you scared to look into the medallion?" asked Ali.

"Yes. But it's the only way," answered Don.

Don held up the medallion and looked deep into the Eye of Horus. Suddenly, the ground seemed to shake. A wind whirled around him, and the torch flames swirled and danced. He seemed to spin into a black emptiness, and then he saw the same huge chamber. Only it looked different. There was no modern equipment for melting gold, no damage from the explosion. The room was empty. A green scarab bowl lay on the floor. Steam rose from it. On the far wall was an opening to a tunnel.

As if in a dream, Don entered the tunnel, and followed it to the burial room. He saw the closed coffin. It was the same coffin he had seen Falcon place the vizier's body in.

"Dono, come back. Talk to me. Where are you?" Ali's voice sounded far away.

"I'm in the burial room. I know how to get there now."

Don struggled back to reality. It seemed to be getting harder and harder to return from the eerie world of the medallion. Don thought with a shudder, what if one time I can't come back?

He shook his head and hurried to the place where he'd seen the opening. It looked like a solid wall.

"Help me find the lever, Ali," Don said.

"There's a tunnel behind this wall that leads directly to the burial room. This place must be honeycombed with tunnels."

It took them a long time to find the lever. But they finally did, and when Don touched the lever, the wall opened up to reveal another tunnel.

"I'll go, Don. You wait here with Ben."

"Thanks, Ali."

Ali flicked on his flashlight and sprinted off down the tunnel. Don returned to Ben's side. He leaned over the still body of his brother, holding the medallion tight in his hand.

"Ben," he whispered, "we're going to have a great time when we get back home. Mom and Dad are the greatest. They're archaeologists, and we'll get to go lots of places with them."

Don searched his twin's face to see if there was any sign that Ben could hear him. There was no change in his death-like face.

"You'll like my friends," Don said, crying softly. Now that he finally had a brother, he was afraid he would slip away forever. "We can share my room. It's a really neat room. I have lots of stuff from all over the world."

As he spoke, he rubbed the medallion without thinking about it. "I'll teach you how to play baseball. I'll teach you everything. It's going to be great, Ben."

What are these things you are talking about?

For a second, Don thought Ben had spoken. But Ben's face was still frozen in the sleep of death. Then Don realized he had heard the words in his head. "Am I going crazy?" he muttered aloud to himself.

What are you doing in my chambers? the voice demanded.

Don whirled around. There stood the ghastly vizier in his yellow robe. His blackened fingers clutched a medallion. His evil yellow eyes bored straight into Don.

Don stood paralyzed with fear, feeling the overwhelming hate from the horrible vizier.

CHAPTER 11

Return to the Tomb of Death

THE hideous thing stared at Don, then at Ben on the marble slab.

Cobra! Falcon! Again Don seemed to hear the words in his head.

The vizier picked up a jeweled knife. He moved slowly toward Don.

"Look," Don said. "I—I'm not a prince. I'm just an American kid."

The vizier touched his medallion. Through the magic of the medallions, he seemed to understand Don's words.

Do not lie! the vizier said angrily. *I know who you both are. I do not know which of you is Cobra, but I thought I had killed him. You must have discovered my potion that brings one back from the dead.*

"Please, don't hurt me. I'm not Falcon or Cobra," Don pleaded. "I'm just Don Hunt."

The vizier's hideous face became twisted

with rage and hate. Each step he took toward Don brought him closer to revenge.

You are Falcon!

Don stumbled backward, trying to escape the relentless advance of the blackened creature. "I'm not Falcon," he babbled, almost insane with fear. "Falcon put you in the coffin 5000 years ago. My friend and I opened the coffin, and some liquid fell on you and brought you back to life."

Silence, puny creature! Lies! Lies! You are the one who made me to look like a hideous monster. You shall pay! I shall have my revenge!

Don fell backward over a pile of jars and landed on the ground. The vizier, his hateful, deformed face gloating in final triumph, lifted his knife. Don saw the yellow teeth and black lips twist into an dreadful smile. The only sound Don heard was his own scream.

Suddenly, through the crater in the wall stepped a mummy. Don saw the icy green eyes and smelled the dank mold. In one hand the mummy carried a small funerary jar. The other arm was stretched out. The mummy limped toward the vizier.

"Cobra!" Don yelled.

The mummy knocked the knife from the stunned vizier's hand, and then picked it up.

The vizier backed into a corner, howling in rage. The mummy struck the vizier, and he fell unconscious in a corner.

The mummy turned and started toward Don. Frozen with fear, Don lay on the ground.

But the mummy stopped and touched the Falcon medallion he was wearing. He pointed to the one Don had around his neck.

Don touched Cobra's medallion and heard these words in his head, *Do not be frightened, my friend. I will not hurt vou.*

The mummy handed Don the knife.

"Wh—where did you come from?"

I have been searching for my tomb, Prince Cobra said. *The mountain no longer looks the same.*

"An explosion blew up the mountain. I don't know if it wrecked your tomb."

The medallion drew me to you. With them, we can understand each other.

"Tell me, what are these medallions? How can we talk to each other?"

Long ago, a huge rock fell from the skies, the mummy explained. *Ahmeket made medallions for me, my brother Falcon, and himself. The rock from the skies had special powers.*

"A meteor from space! It was you who saved me out on the desert, wasn't it?" said Don. "You carried me back to camp?"

The mummy nodded. *I wanted no harm to come to you. You helped me once.* The mummy held up the small funerary jar. *You gave me back my heart that*—he pointed to the vizier who was lying as if dead in the corner—*that miserable creature took from me.*

The mummy took the medallion from around his neck and held it out to Don. *Farewell, my friend,* he said. *I will keep searching for my tomb. If I can find it, I will be able to rest in peace.*

Don took the medallion from the 5000-year-old mummy. The mummy studied Don's face for a moment longer, as if trying to remember what he himself had looked like so many years ago. Then he turned and disappeared through the opening in the wall.

Don stared after the mummy. He was rubbing his eyes, wondering if it all had really happened, when Ali appeared in the tunnel from the burial room. At the sight of the vizier crumpled in the corner, Ali stopped in his tracks.

"Don! It's him!"

"Did you get the bottle?"

Ali held it up.

"Splash the stuff on Ben's face—quick!"

Suddenly, they heard a loud cracking sound. Sand, rock, and rubble from the damaged ceiling began to fall. Ali rushed to Ben's side and sprinkled the last of the vizier's potion on the pale face.

Almost immediately, Ben's eyes opened. He saw them and sat up.

Ben muttered something in Arabic. Then he added in English, "What happened? Where am I?"

From behind them they heard a howl of anger. Spinning around they saw that Ahmeket had stood up and was stumbling toward them, his yellow eyes on fire with hate.

"Let's get out of here!" Don cried. "The place is caving in."

He put the Cobra medallion around Ben's neck and the Falcon one around his own. "Hurry!"

The three of them rushed to the chamber door. Another loud crash filled the room with dust and rock. Don turned to see the vizier standing amid the falling rubble.

"Ali, get your camera and take a picture of him!" Don shouted above the roar of the collapsing mountain. "Then we can prove he was really here."

Ali snapped the picture as rock and dirt fell around them. "I hope this is a good one," he said as they ran down the tunnel that led past the traps to where Grandpa Pete was waiting for them.

"Are you okay? Can you make it?" Don asked his brother.

"I am fine. I feel as if I have had a long rest."

"Do you still have the rope and the hook, Ali? We'll need them to get over the pits," Don said after they had been running for a few minutes.

"Yep," Ali replied.

The three of them raced along the passageway, making their way past the traps.

They stopped to rest a safe distance away from the collapsing center of the mountain.

"Ben, what happened to you?" Don asked. "Did Abdul hurt you?"

"No," Ben answered. "He took me into that chamber and tied me up. That's a secret place where he had his equipment for melting down the gold. Then he left. I must have gotten sick because I had a terrible nightmare. A man who was all black and shriveled-up forced me to drink something. It tasted awful. I don't remember any more. But I think he wasn't a bad dream, was he? He was there in the chamber."

"Yeah," answered Don. "He was there. He tried to kill me. Wait a minute! Ali! Let's see that picture you took."

They waited breathlessly as Ali pulled the photo out of his camera. But all the photo showed was a blur of yellow and black in the dusty chamber.

"You can't really tell much," Don said with disappointment.

"I think I can see his eyes, but they're not very clear," added Ben.

"It looks as bad as all my pictures," Ali said in disgust. "I should have practiced more with the camera."

"There was someone else in the room," explained Don. "When Ali went to the burial room for the potion, Cobra the mummy showed up! He—he saved my life. He was also the one who carried me back to camp when Abdul kidnapped me."

"But where did this medallion come from?" asked Ben. "Now there are two."

"It's from the mummy, Ben. Now we each have one."

They heard a faraway rumbling in the center of the mountain. "Come on," said Ali. "Rest time is over. We better get going."

"One more thing," said Don. "I think we should wait for the right time to tell what happened. People won't believe us. Let's not say anything right away—okay?"

Ben and Ali agreed that that was a good idea. In a short time they came to the cage trap. Don showed Ben the raised areas that triggered the cage, and they stepped carefully around them. Soon they came to the snake pit. They shined their lights across on Grandpa Pete, who had heard them coming and was watching anxiously.

"Thank goodness you're safe!" he cried. "It sounds like the heavy rains have made the mountain cave in where it was weakened from the explosion. Hey, is that Ben with you?"

"Yes! He's safe, Grandpa!" shouted Don.

Grandpa Pete struggled to his feet and said, "Use the hook and rope, and swing on over. But don't look in the pit, boys. Promise me."

"Uh, sure. We promise," answered Don. "But why?"

"I'll tell you when you're over."

The boys made it over the pit with no trouble. Don was tempted to shine his flashlight down at the snake, but he kept his promise to his grandfather. So did Ali and Ben.

They all hugged Grandpa Pete. They were interrupted by a tremendous crash further inside the mountain. A stream of dust came through the tunnel.

"Uh-oh," said Grandpa Pete. "Those cave-ins are getting closer. Let's skedaddle. You can tell me everything later when we're safe."

They took turns helping Grandpa Pete to

walk, and they made slow time. They managed to stay one step ahead of the cave-ins behind them, but there was no time to waste. At last they came to the final pit, the one with the stakes in it. They threw the rope and hook across and swung over to safety.

They burst out of the open tunnel door and collapsed on rocks in the bright sunshine. They all had to cover their eyes for several minutes before they were used to the sun.

Ali was the first to speak. "Why couldn't we look into the snake pit?"

"I didn't want you to see what was in there," Grandpa Pete answered. "I was resting where you left me when I heard someone running madly down the tunnel you had gone down. I didn't know who it was, but the screams were something I'll never forget. They were the screams of someone who had seen something we humans were not meant to see."

"I shined my flashlight down the tunnel. As the person got closer, I could make out some of the words he was yelling in Arabic. Then I saw Abdul with a terrified look on his face, racing like a madman straight toward the snake pit. He barely looked human. I tried to warn him, but he fell straight into the pit. Then I heard a hissing sound and a blood-chilling scream, and I knew that was the end of our friend the grave robber."

The boys were silent after hearing the story of Abdul's terrible end. Don noticed that Ben looked sad and thoughtful. He put his hand on his brother's shoulder.

"I know he was a terrible man, and treated me like a slave," said Ben softly. "But still he was the only family I had."

"Well, now we are your family," Don said.

Then Ali asked, "What was Abdul saying, Grandpa Hunt?"

"Well, he sounded hysterical, and he kept repeating the words, *The blackened thing, the horrible blackened thing—Allah save me from the blackened thing.* I can't make anything out of it."

Don looked at Ali and Ben. They said nothing about the vizier.

"Let's wait until later in the day when it's cooler to start back to the village," said Grandpa Pete. They rested a while longer, listening to the booms and crashes from the collapsing center of the mountain.

Don realized that Ali was very quiet. Don touched his friend's arm. "We never would have found Ben without you," he said. "Thanks."

"I wouldn't have missed it for anything," Ali answered. Then he grinned. "Only I don't know how I'll ever be able to put up with two of you!"

As they were about to go to the place where Don had hidden the donkeys, Don and Ben touched their medallions at the same time and looked at each other.

Nothing will ever keep us apart again, said Don.

Ben smiled and nodded.

But then a darkness seemed to fill Don's mind. Something evil was creeping in. He glanced at his brother and saw by his troubled face that Ben felt it, too. Then words filled his mind.

Falcon! Cobra! You will never escape me. Wherever you go, I will find you. I will find you and gain my revenge!

About the Author

ALIDA E. YOUNG and her husband live in the high desert of southern California. She gets many of her ideas by talking with people. She's tried to learn to listen—not just to what people say, but to how they say it. When she's writing a book that requires research, she talks to experts. "Everyone is so helpful," she says. "They go out of their way to help."

Mrs. Young has visited archaeological digs in Egypt, Italy, and Greece. One of her childhood dreams was to be an archaeologist, but she never expected to see the Pyramids or King Tut's tomb. While in Cairo, she stayed at the Tulip Hotel. She walked through the bazaars and the ancient sections of the city.

Other books by Alida Young include *Megan the Klutz*, *Why am I Too Young*, *What's Wrong With Daddy?*, *The Klutz Strikes Again*, *I Never Got to Say Good-bye*, and *Summer Cruise, Summer Love.*